Cat Heaven

written and illustrated by

CYNTHIA RYLANT

THE BLUE SKY PRESS
An Imprint of Scholastic Inc. · New York

FOR CAPS, NICK, ,

AND

EDWARD VELVETPAWS

The way to Cat Heaven

is a field of sweet grass

where crickets

and butterflies play.

A cat may be late in getting to Heaven...

there's just so much fun on the way!

But an angel will wait
at the yellow front door,
wait till a kitty
comes home.

And when she arrives,
he'll give her a kiss
and some milk
in a bowl of her own.

There are trees
in Cat Heaven,
trees made
just for cats,
trees growing
so green and so high.

But no one
gets stuck
in a tree
anymore—
if a cat
wants down,
she will fly!

And oh, all the toys,

kitty toys everywhere,

thousands and thousands

go by.

There are angels,

of course,

with soft angel laps

where kitties can purr

loud and strong.

The angels will rub

kitties' noses and ears

and sing them

a Cat Heaven song.

And when cats are hungry,
there's God's kitchen counter

all covered with
white kitty dishes,
full of tuna and salmon
and mounds of sardines,
and wonderful little pink fishes.

The cats in Cat Heaven
are so loved and spoiled

God lets them all
lie on His bed....

He walks
in His garden
with a good black book

and a kitty

asleep on His head.

Then when a cat needs,

she may just simply ponder

and watch the blue world deep and wide....

She will watch the old house
where she once lived and wandered,
and the people
who loved her inside.

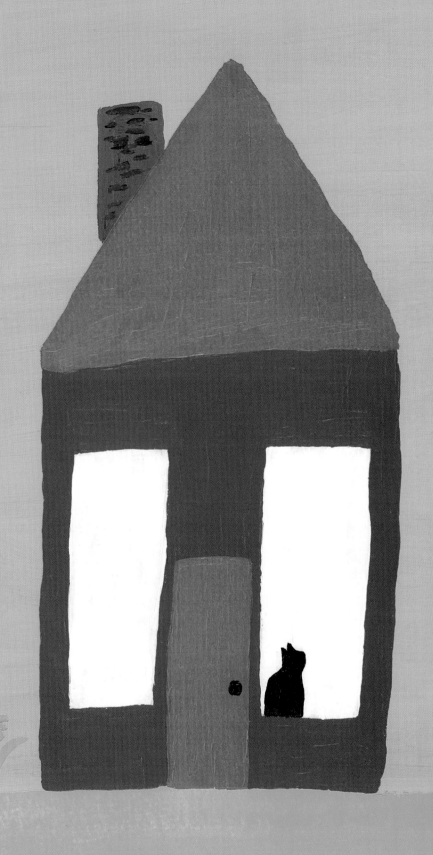

All cats love Heaven,
they know the way there,

they know where
the angel cats fly.

They'll run past the stars

and the moon and the sun. . .

...to curl up with God in the sky.

THE BLUE SKY PRESS

Copyright © 1997 by Cynthia Rylant

For information regarding permission, please write to:
Permissions Department,
Scholastic Inc., 557 Broadway, New York, New York 10012.

SCHOLASTIC, THE BLUE SKY PRESS, and associated logos
are trademarks and/or registered trademarks of Scholastic Inc.

Library of Congress catalog card number: 96049501

ISBN-13: 978-0-590-10054-0 / ISBN-10: 0-590-10054-8

40 39 38 37 36 35 34 33 32 31   16/0

Printed in Malaysia   108

First printing, September 1997